The Perfect Princess & the Bog Monster

The Perfect Princess & the Bog Monster

ABC
Books

Published by ABC Books for the
AUSTRALIAN BROADCASTING CORPORATION
GPO Box 9994 Sydney NSW 2001

First published 2005

National Library of Australia
Cataloguing-in-Publication entry
The perfect princess and the bog monster: tall and twisted fairy
tales from Aussie kids.

For children aged eight and over.

ISBN 0 7333 1688 3.

1. Fairy tales – Australia. 2. Children's writings, Australian.
I. Vane, Mitch. II. Australian Broadcasting Corporation.

A823.40803523

Edited by Jody Lee
Illustrated by Mitch Vane
Designed by Fisheye Design
Set in Stempel Schneidler 11.5/16pt
Colour reproduction by Graphic Print Group, Adelaide
Printed and bound by Griffin Press, Adelaide

The publisher would like to thank the following organisations for
their support of this project: ABC Television, the Royal Danish
Consulate in Sydney, Finnesse Communications Marketing &
PR, the Hans Christian Andersen 2005 Foundation and the Hans
Christian Andersen abc Foundation.

HANS CHRISTIAN ANDERSEN abc FOUNDATION

Contents

Foreword   6

The Perfect Princess   8

The Brightest Butterfly   13

The Cursed Kimono   16

The Locket   22

The Beautiful Laugh   26

The Well-Dressed, Peckish Princess
& the Kamikaze Leaping Mouse   30

Sunshine   35

Lord Brazzal of Sprat & his
Onion & Potato   40

A Fruity Fairytale   45

The Painter   51

Scorchio the Dragon   55

Princess Plum's Prophecy   58

The Very Plain Egg   63

Rose   68

Heroes in Disguise   74

The Princess Who Was Different   80

The Troll's Bride   85

The Little Doll   88

A True Fairy Tail   92

Foreword
by HRH Crown Princess Mary of Denmark

As Honorary Hans Christian Andersen Ambassador to Australia it is both an honour and a pleasure to see all these wonderful stories from ABC TV's Hans Christian Andersen Story Competition being published. This book, together with the celebrations of Hans Christian Andersen in Australia and worldwide, will promote a wider awareness and appreciation of, as well as honour, this great Danish storyteller.

I would like to take this opportunity to sincerely thank the organisers of ABC TV's Hans Christian Andersen Story Competition. This event has led to the production of this beautiful book which gives others the chance to enjoy the many funny, warm and wonderfully creative stories inspired by the fairytales of Hans Christian Andersen.

In particular, I wish to emphasise the importance of humanitarian foundations such as the Hans Christian Andersen abc Foundation whose aim is to support the problem of illiteracy across the world. According to UNESCO, there are more than one billion illiterate people worldwide—15% of which are children.

This book is a worthy demonstration of the importance for children to learn how to read and write. These children are the real 'ambassadors' for the fight against illiteracy. They show us all what literacy can bring to life—stories full of joy, wit and love.

The children present a different approach to Hans Christian Andersen's fairytales, but still they adapt the Andersen way of grasping life and a little of life's meaning. Just one example is how insightfully the winner of the story competition, Taeyn, ends his story *The Perfect Princess:*

'So even though your son or daughter might not fit the mould,
Or be the perfect princess as in other stories told.
Their hearts of gold can shine through when you least expect it,
Just give time, here's a hint: prepare to accept it.'

The Perfect Princess

When I wrote the story, I wanted it to be funny.
I don't know any kid who doesn't like gross
things, scary characters, and happy endings. I
always like rhyming stories, because I find them
easy and fun to read. Some of the characters in my
story, I have met, and some of the animals, I have
known or seen. Yes, I have been drooled on by a
camel, and my rabbit chewed through anything
left on the floor. I loved writing this story and
hope that you like it too.

Taeyn, age 10

There was a happy princess with a glowing smile,
She had a pet lizard and a crocodile.
Her love of the strange concerned her mum and dad,
Everything she liked was either ugly, gross or bad.

She had a dog that had no teeth, so she fed him
    baby food.
She had a farting cat, isn't that **rude**.
She loved her drooling camels, although they drool
    everywhere.
One glob of drool had landed in her mother's hair.
Her mum and dad were at a loss. What could they do?
They had to get her interested in something new.

The Queen asked her daughter to come out to the garden,
And take some time out from her animals who couldn't
    say pardon.
'But doesn't digging in the dirt mean I could get germs …
Oh, how cute, a family of **slimy** worms!'

They took her clothes shopping to stop her nasty habit,
They walked the streets for fashion and came home with
    a rabbit.
The rabbit pooped everywhere, the nasty little brute,
And gnawed a little hole in the King's new boot.

The King put his shoe on the very next day,
His daughter's mice had moved in and filled the shoe
    with hay.
'I've had more than enough!' the King yelled in disgust,
'She has to find a hobby that we can trust.

No more creepy animals, no more nasty poos,
No more horrid mice in my brand new shoes!'

But then something happened, a shock for **all of** us,
A creature had arrived on the 'Number 16' bus.
'**A bOg monster!**' the people cried, it gave them an
  awful fright,
It arrived around nine p.m. on a Friday night.

'We'll have to send an army, that's all that we can do,
We'll frighten him and rid the land of his disgusting goo.
He's heading for the castle, send the men out quick,
Pinch him, poke him, anything. Heck, hit him with
  a stick.'

The monster approached the castle walls, eating everything
  in sight,
The army threw some tennis balls, to him they were
  Turkish Delight.
'I've run out of ideas,' the worried King said,
'I guess we'll have to pack our bags or we'll end
  up dead.'

'**wAIT!**' cried the Princess, 'I have an idea,
I think I've got a way to get the monster out of here.
I have a lot of animals, that much is true,
But I could love a bog monster and my animals, too.
I bet he wants our love, I bet he wants a cuddle,
That will get us out of this **terrible muddle!**'

The King sighed, exhausted, 'You know perhaps she's right,
Our army is too tired to stay and fight.'

'There is a place not far from here I'm sure that he
   will love.'
It was as if a lightning bolt had come from up above.
The Princess ran to the castle walls and gave the monster
   a thump,
'How'd you like to take a trip to the garbage dump?

'It's like a café for monsters, with food and drink galore,
And when you've had enough to eat then you can eat
   some more.
It's lovely and **gooey** and **grimy**. It's my favourite
   place to be,
And I'll come around on Saturday for a nice cup of tea.'
The monster's eyes filled with tears, 'You mean you'll be
   my friend?'
'Not only that,' the Princess cried. 'I'll be there 'til the end!'

The King and Queen stopped and stared in utter disbelief,
Their daughter had tamed the beast, what a huge relief.
The monster was leaving, the kingdom was fine,
They had won the battle in the nick of time.

The Princess had succeeded in saving the land,
Not with an army, but with a friendly hand.
Who said battles could be won with fighting?
This battle was over and ended with uniting.
They had a new friend, and ally, a pal,
All thanks to their grimy but **special** **little** **gal**.

The monster thought his new home was a beautiful treat,
With all the garbage available a monster could eat.

He'd never been happier, his life was amazing,
He had his new friend, and was forever found grazing.
If ever there was a recycling problem he would solve it.
Eating and drinking rubbish, he just dissolved it.

The kingdom was happier than it had ever been,
And the Princess's parents were the proudest to be seen.
They didn't mind the mess, the stink from all those
    grimy mammals,
The farting cat, the toothless dog, the constantly
    drooling camels.
So even though your son or daughter might not fit
    the mould,
Or be the perfect princess as in other stories told,
Their hearts of gold can shine through when you least
    expect it,
Just give them time, here's a hint: prepare to accept it.

The King and Queen looked at each other, the problem
    was out of the way,
Although it was a rather nasty, horrid kind of day.
We've learned to love our little girl, her grime is no longer
    a barrier.
The problem is to find a charming prince prepared to
    marry her.

The End

The Brightest Butterfly

'The Brightest Butterfly' was originally written for a home-school project on butterflies.

I live on a bushland property in a beautiful valley. In summertime there are always butterflies in the garden attracted by the bright flowering plants—it seems to me that butterflies and colour go together!

I love colour, I like wearing blue jeans and hot-pink t-shirts, snuggling under my patchwork quilt and admiring the colours of nature from my window.

Imagine a world without colour, it would be so terribly boring!

I wrote this story to remind people that we all need colour in our lives.

Michaela, age 10

Once upon a time, in a place far away, lived a butterfly. His name was Benjamin and he was the brightest butterfly in the garden.

He had spotted wings—big black spots on an orange background—streaked with red, yellow, green, blue, indigo and violet: all the colours of the rainbow. He was very bright indeed!

Benjamin's garden had been planted by Beryl, a grey-haired lady who didn't like colours that clashed. She was afraid to use colour and chose only to plant white flowers; anyway, all the gardening magazines said that white was 'ever so fashionable'. In her garden were roses, daisies, lilies, daffodils (white varieties, of course), so many flowers but all were white.

'I wish rainbow flowers grew in my garden,' sighed Benjamin. 'All the flowers in my garden are so plain.' In his dreams he saw a garden filled with bright flowers overflowing with enticing, sweet nectar.

What Benjamin didn't know was that the white flowers would one day turn into rainbow flowers. All that was needed was a lovely spring day, a shower of rain, a ray of sunshine and a little **magic**.

The magic could only work after a drought and that year no rain fell. The flowers faded and drooped but were still alive, waiting for the magic.

Butterflies live for a few short weeks, but Benjamin lived on, his colours as bright as ever. Perhaps it was the magic that kept him alive, or maybe it was his hopes and dreams.

Benjamin had been looking for nectar when it began to rain. Magically, streaks of red, orange, yellow, blue, indigo and violet were appearing on the petals. Colourful birds, bees and insects started to arrive, drawn to the colours and the promise of nectar. As miraculous as his own metamorphosis, the garden was being transformed, colour was bringing life, abundant life, into the garden.

Beryl was in the garden that day and had been caught in the shower. She was about to go inside when she noticed streaks of colour running down the petals, blending together.

'**Beautiful**,' she gasped. She stood and watched as blossoms on the trees changed from white to pink, and if you looked closely you could see tinges of blue, indigo and violet.

Beryl didn't know what had taken place that day, but it felt good. As she turned around she saw her reflection in the kitchen window; her grey hair was now a shade of orange streaked with gold, even indigo and violet.

'Beautiful,' she smiled to herself.

And Benjamin the brightest butterfly now lived in the brightest garden, a beautiful garden of colour.

The End

The Cursed Kimono

Late last year in drama class, we were asked to do an improvisation for a play with only a phrase to work from. My group's phrase was 'The Cursed Kimono' and after a quick brainstorm and performance, the phrase remained in my head.

Early in 2005 when The Hans Christian Andersen fairytale competition was announced, I remembered 'The Cursed Kimono' and welcomed the opportunity to put my ideas together and write my interpretation of the story. As I have always enjoyed fairytales, I found it exciting and pleasurable to be writing one of my own. I hope you enjoy my tale!

Adam, age 14

Once upon a time, there was a forest to the north of Japan. Passers-by would look at the tall, dark trees and walk by, as they could not see what lay beyond the clustered woods. In the very centre of the forest was a waterfall. Although the waterfall was magnificent, it was what lay behind the waterfall that was special. If you were to walk into the dark cave behind that waterfall, you would discover the most beautiful sight. Encircled by forbidding mountains was a valley with a little town, a castle made of gold, and the most beautiful gardens that would take you a lifetime to explore. But the most beautiful thing in this secret valley wasn't the town or the castle or the gardens. It was the Princess, and this tale is about her.

Princess Miroshiki woke up to the early morning birdcalls and could not feel happier. Today she was picking her Ceremonial Wedding Kimono. Tailors from far and wide brought their most prized kimonos for the Princess to judge. It would be a great honour for the tailor if the Princess chose their gown for her wedding.

Princess Miroshiki headed down to the Great Hall, where she would choose her kimono.

Miroshiki made her way down the line of tailors displaying their prized work. She remarked on each kimono and selected several favoured gowns to be taken for fitting in the dressing-room. She came to the last tailor and commented, 'I'm sorry, but the colour of this kimono reminds me of dirt.'

'Actually, it's a new colour specially made for your gown; it's called mud brown,' said the tailor.

'I'm sorry, it is too dull,' said Miroshiki.

Thanking the tailors, Princess Miroshiki departed.

Yojella, the travelling tailor, had never felt so insulted in all her life. She angrily muttered, 'Miroshiki thinks she is so wonderful. I want revenge. Perhaps the dreaded witch who lives near the mountain can help.'

* * ✳ * *

Darkness had fallen when she reached the witch's home. She knocked at the door and a sharp screech answered, 'What do you want, Stranger?'

'My name is Yojella, I seek revenge on Miroshiki!'

With a loud creak, the door opened to reveal an exceedingly unpleasant-looking old woman.

'Come in, my dear, and tell me all your troubles.'

The witch and Yojella discussed their hatred for the Princess Miroshiki. Suddenly the witch cackled, 'I have the perfect revenge! Take this potion and pour it on Miroshiki's Ceremonial Wedding Kimono. When she puts it on, she will die. She will never enter the afterlife as **she will not be able to remove the Cursed Kimono!**'

Travelling through the night, Yojella finally reached the castle. Climbing through an open window, she stealthily headed towards the dressing-room. When she entered, she found the chosen kimono lying on a velvet-covered table. She quickly poured the witch's potion on the kimono. It glowed an acid green for a second, then turned back into its original colour. Yojella quickly left the castle and fled the valley.

The next morning, Miroshiki excitedly rushed to see her Ceremonial Wedding Kimono again. She couldn't resist trying it on and slipped it over her shoulders. Immediately, she fell to the floor and moved no more.

The news of the Princess's death spread quickly. The Princess was buried beside the lake in the Royal Garden, where a memorial was erected.

The townspeople were so devastated they eventually all left the valley.

Over time, the town and the castle were destroyed by storms and neglect but the garden remained, protected by the Princess's spirit.

Years later, a young man named Moko was keen to discover what secrets lay within the North Forest of Japan. As he walked through the forest it got darker and colder. Eventually he stumbled upon a waterfall. While having a drink, he saw the cave.

'Let's see where this cave leads to.' He walked through and was amazed at what he found. A beautiful garden spanned out across a large valley; next to it was a blue lake.

As he reached the lake, he was severely startled. A lady dressed in a beautiful kimono was hovering above the ground. Moko turned to run, but before he could, the lady cried, 'Please help me. I am trapped in this garden for all eternity if no one helps.'

'What must I do?' asked Moko quietly.

'Between the tallest mountains is a gorge where a small hut lies. The witch who cursed my kimono may still have a potion to reverse the spell. Bring back the potion and I will be free of this curse. You should be safe as the witch should be long gone.'

Moko hurried towards the gorge.

* * ❋ * *

Arriving in the gorge, Moko saw smoke coming from the chimney of a small, stone house carved into the mountain.

'This looks like the witch's house the woman in the kimono described. However, she should be dead.' Moko cautiously entered the house.

There was a cauldron bubbling away in the middle of the house. The contents smelt foul.

'**Aha!**' screamed a voice behind him. 'Finally. Someone to cook in my human soup!'

A long purple bolt of lightning came out of a crooked wand the witch was holding. Moko dodged and ran for cover behind the cauldron.

'What can I do?' he thought desperately.

He glanced to his right and saw the lid of the cauldron.

'Prepare to be soup!' cackled the witch.

She fired a red bolt but before it hit Moko, he protected himself with the lid. The bolt rebounded and hit the witch.

'**NOOOOO!!!**' cried the witch. With that she turned into a bowl of red, fleshy soup, which broke on impact with the floor and quickly dissolved into the dust. Moko discovered a small cupboard labelled **Potions** and opened it. There were so many to choose from: **Wart Remover, Death Carrier, Hair Grower**.

Finally he came upon a blue potion labelled **Curse Remover**.

Triumphantly he grabbed the potion and headed down through the gorge to the woman in the kimono.

'I found it!' exclaimed Moko. 'But first, please tell me your name.'

'My name is Miroshiki. I am Princess of this land.'

'Thank you,' said Moko and handed Miroshiki the potion.

Taking the potion, Miroshiki poured it over her kimono. A look of relief showed on her tired face.

'Thank you, Moko. My spirit is free and I will depart for the afterlife, but before I go …'

Miroshiki picked one of the roses from the garden and placed it in Moko's hand. With that the Princess and the garden all evaporated into the still air and left Moko alone in the valley.

* * ✳ * *

The moral of this tale is, by helping somebody, the rewards can be simple or great. The greatest reward is knowing you have their eternal gratitude.

The End

The Locket

When I saw the first ad on TV for the competition, I couldn't stop thinking about all the possibilities. I tried to focus on how Princess Mary and Prince Frederik would be coming to Australia shortly and I wanted to include something of European origin in the fairytale. I therefore included European names.

When watching the news that night, I saw some depressing images of war, terror and famine. I started thinking about people who weren't so lucky, people who didn't have their whole family with them.

I try to look on the bright side of life, but it is often hard to do in situations like this. It is important to remember loved ones and find something, an event or a time, to trigger happy memories. Heinz's locket brought back happy memories that he can treasure forever.

Christina, age 12

A little boy stared at a picture of his mother, very curious, so very deep in sadness.

'What was she like?' he asked his father.

'Never you mind!' his father shouted, making his poor son's heart flinch with fear.

The boy stared out the window, watching his father weep about his lost love.

* * ✳ * *

Heinz was a good boy. He would be strong, he wouldn't cry, although his feelings grew more intense, more sincere whenever he thought of his mother's sun-kissed skin he had never touched.

He slowly walked to his room to fetch his hat and sack for work. The boy reached into his pocket for the most treasured thing he owned. It was a locket which, Johanna, his mother, had kept for him. Inside it were two words, 'Johanna' and 'loves'. There was no sign of a third word; it had probably been worn away through time, Heinz assumed.

As he picked berries, he thought about what could have been if his mother were still alive. It would have been magic. Johanna would have taught him how to speak to the animals and helped him understand even the most difficult of times. When his fantasy came to an end, he knew deep inside his heart that there was **no hope of magic**.

Heinz started to cry uncontrollably. Gold tears ran down his innocent face and made a large puddle on the ground. It was as if he was meant to cry.

An old man squatted beside him and stared. He said nothing. For minutes, there was pure silence. Heinz felt like he had known this old man forever. There was no need for words, there was just a silent understanding. The old man whispered softly, 'Johanna loves.' Heinz stared back in disbelief and with trust in his eyes.

'**Go where it shines, and the sun will dry your tears**. You will never be sad again,' preached the old man. Then he picked up his bag and left ever so quietly.

The boy wished the old man would stay. Heinz was so lonely. What did the old man mean? Heinz already knew that the warmth of the sun could dry your tears, but what use was this to him?

Heinz dropped his belongings and ran, ran as fast as he could, towards the sun.

'Mother!' he called out. 'Where are you?' The sun shone warm upon his little face as the gold tears beaded down his pale cheeks. The warm gold of the sun replaced his tears with red cheeks. It felt like kisses.

He opened the locket.

'Thank you for this, Mother, it means so much to me.' Silence again. There was no one there; he was alone. Heinz looked at his locket, unfulfilled and disappointed. There were the words, 'Johanna' and 'loves'.

'As it always has been and always will!' he shouted. Heinz read the inscription again. There was the name 'Heinz', as it should have been, as if it had always been!

The sun kissed his cheeks, almost like a loving mother kissing her son. He knew that the locket would always stay the same, and he kept it close to his heart. 'Johanna loves Heinz', he read again.

The End

The Beautiful Laugh

I wrote my story about a princess who isn't very pretty because I thought that if I wrote about a normal princess, I would not know what to say. I wanted the princess to be very different from the others, so I gave her a beautiful laugh. I wanted to have a girl who has something special about them other than good looks.

I chose the flute at the start of her laugh because I play the flute and I think it has a lovely sound. I wanted my story to make people feel that you don't have to have good looks to be special.

Romy, age 9

Many years ago, a tiny princess lived in a humble cottage with her parents, who were the King and Queen of a small island known as Kertin. The Princess was called Pixie because she was so small. The little Princess did not have good looks. Her hair was cropped short and it was a dull, mousy colour. Her little face was elf-like and a long, pointy nose in the middle of her face looked like a little carrot had been placed there, except that it was skin-coloured.

The young Princess knew she wasn't pretty, but she did have the most **beautiful laugh** anyone had ever heard. She laughed often. She was quite a happy girl and saw the funny side to so many things. When she saw something funny, her mouth would open up and the most lovely sound would fill the whole room.

It was like a flute to begin with, then other instruments would join in, but in a **laughter sort of melody**. People stopped and stood still, listening to her, and then they would join in laughing and smiling. Pixie's mum and dad loved to hear her laugh because she made their household so happy.

All the servants would hum and sing and laugh too when they heard the little girl laugh. Everyone was happy, except on some days when Pixie wasn't. She would look into her bedroom mirror and wish she was pretty. She would smile at her image and see her crooked teeth and funny nose. She wished her hair was blonde and long, maybe even a bit curly. But then a beetle would appear on her dressing table and get stuck on his back, his little legs kicking and fighting, trying to flip over, and she would start to laugh. Of course she would help him turn over, but once her laughter had started she soon forgot that she wasn't pretty.

A Prince from the village called Mistyl heard people talk about the Princess and her beautiful laugh, and he announced that he would like to meet her right away. Other village women had told him that she did not have good looks so there was no point in going, but the Prince did not care. He wanted to meet a princess who wasn't into looking at herself in a mirror all day long. He wanted a happy princess who liked having fun. All the soldiers got the Prince's biggest boat ready so they could set sail. The next day, the boat got to the little island known as Kertin. It seemed like a beautiful island. The Prince and his soldiers travelled around and they saw many people laughing and dancing, so they joined in. While dancing, they stopped still to listen to a beautiful noise coming from a cottage. It sounded like a flute playing, then all the other instruments would join in, but in a **laughter sort of melody**.

The Prince looked into a little window and saw what was making the lovely noise. He and his soldiers walked up to the cottage door and knocked loudly. A maid opened the door and said 'Come in,' when the Prince announced who he was. The Prince asked the maid where the Princess's room was.

'Oh, she sleeps at the end room on the right.'

The Prince went to the room and knocked. The door opened a crack and a little pointy nose poked out.

'Excuse me, but are you Princess Pixie?' asked the Prince.

'I am,' said a tiny voice.

'Could we meet?' said the Prince, wondering why she wasn't showing herself.

'This evening by the lilypond at the bottom of our garden,' Pixie said.

The Prince left feeling a little disappointed, but evening came around quickly. The Prince was very nervous as he waited by the lilypond. He looked up when he heard tiny footsteps.

A small, veiled girl stood before him.

'Is that you, Princess Pixie?' he asked in surprise. He stepped back and fell right into the pond.

The little flute started, then the other instruments followed. Pixie was laughing and she couldn't stop. She reached over and helped the Prince to climb out of the pond. He was soaked but realised how funny he must have looked. He started to laugh and the two fell about laughing and crying with happiness. Pixie's veil had fallen off and the Prince didn't notice that she wasn't pretty. All he could do was laugh with her, and that was how he fell in love with a beautiful laughing Princess. They married and their whole lives were happy because they always laughed and loved their life together.

The End

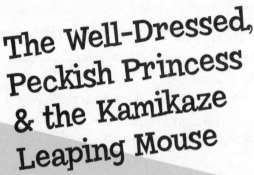

The Well-Dressed, Peckish Princess & the Kamikaze Leaping Mouse

My fairytale, 'The Well-Dressed, Peckish Princess & the Kamikaze Leaping Mouse', was inspired by many things. Escaping pet rats, a dramatic little sister and guys at school were all inspiration. It was actually my sister who made me write the story. She heard about the competition and decided to write a story. I thought that if she won, I'd kick myself for not entering. So I did.

I decided that the 'hero' of the story had to be a mouse for they are highly underrated animals when it comes to fairytales. The story basically flowed from one idea to another.

Rohana, age 13

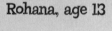

Once upon a time, in a land far, far away, lived a fair princess. Her name was Gertrude. On Friday nights she liked to go to the movies with her boyfriend, Bartholomew.

One day Bartholomew and Princess Gertrude were walking through the lollipop forest when they came upon a house made out of Fantales.

'**Yum!!!**' yelled Bartholomew.

'Why, I do feel rather peckish and it is two hours 'til tea, so let's have a bite,' said Gertrude enthusiastically.

They rushed up to the house and just as they were about to sink their teeth into the delicious caramel goodness ...

'**Oi**, what do you think you are doing?' exclaimed an angry voice. 'Do you think my house is for eating? Would you like it if I turned up to your house and tried to bite it? Huh, what do you say to that?'

'We're awfully sorry, whoever you are. It looked so yummy,' Gertrude tried to explain.

'Don't get all soppy with me. I'm going to lock you in my dungeon made of iron and steel so you can't get out. **Ma ha ha ha haaaaaaaaaa!**' ma ha ha haaaed the voice.

'Who are you?' asked Bartholomew.

A figure stepped out of the house.

'Boo! I am the one, the only witch. Well, actually, there is another one down the road but that's beside the point. Come with me, missy,' she demanded as she pulled Gertrude into the Fantale house.

'I'll be back for you in a minute,' she added to

Bartholomew, who stood with a bemused look on his face.

After what was a minute she returned from locking Gertrude in the dungeon.

'Banana washing machine dishwasher purple monkey good **TOAD!**' the witch yelled. With a blinding flash Bartholomew turned into a toad.

'Hey, Mrs Witch Lady, could you possibly turn me into a mouse? I would be much cuter,' asked Bartholomew.

'Fine, if that's how you want it. Banana peanut butter sandwich computer virus duck orange bikini **MOUSE!**'

And with another blinding flash, Bartholomew the toad turned into a white mouse. Then the witch disappeared.

'Yes,' thought Bartholomew. 'I look much nicer than a toad. Right, concentrate. I'd better go see how Gertrude is.' And so he did.

Gertrude was in a hysterical state. Her mascara was running down her face and her hair was all messy.

'I'm hungry!' she screamed. 'Why couldn't that witch have left me some food?!'

Right then, Bartholomew noticed a small mouse-sized hole in the door.

'**Brilliant!**' he thought. 'I'll bring her food through the hole!'

But if he wanted to take big things to her he had to cut them up and being a mouse that was very hard to do. And it did have to fit through the mouse hole in the door. But he managed to do it.

After Bartholomew had given the Princess enough food he went for a leisurely stroll around the house he was in. On his walk he met many other mice who all knew where the key to the door was.

So Bartholomew headed off on his dangerous journey to the witch's bedroom. It took a good few hours to get up the stairs. When he reached the top, he found that the bedroom door was open. The only problem was that the witch was sitting on her bed happily reading *Witch Weekly*. Stealthily he snuck under the bed to the desk. He opened the drawer with great difficulty, grabbed the key and just as he was about to leave …

'What do you think you're doing, little mousey?' said the witch as she rolled up her magazine. Bartholomew took a kamikaze leap off the desk and scuttled under the bed.

'You can run, but you can't hide,' whispered the witch.

'Wait for the right moment, wait for the right moment,' thought Bartholomew. After a few minutes the witch got bored of threatening the mouse and forgot he had the key. Bartholomew took his chance and ran for the door. Bartholomew shot down the stairs like a bullet out of a gun. He skilfully slid through the hole in the door with ease.

'What have you got now, mouse?' demanded a frustrated Getrude.

'**Eeekkkk**, eeek eek eeeeeeeeek eeek eek eeeeeek eek ek!' eeked Bartholomew, which translated to 'I've got the key to the door so you can escape!'

'A key. Am I right in guessing it's for the door?' asked a slightly less frustrated Gertrude.

'Ekkk ekkk eeeeek eeeeeeeek eek ek ek ek ek ekkk!' eeked Bartholomew, which translated to 'No, it's just a pendant for you. Of course it's for the door!!'

'I'll try it, shall I?' said Gertrude as she walked to the door.

The door sprung open as soon as the key was turned, well, that was when Gertrude realised which way to turn the key. Gertrude ran out of the house, making sure she took a huge bite out of the Fantale brick.

'Thank you, little mouse, you're my hero!' and with that she popped a kiss on the cheek of the mouse.

POOOOFFFFFFF!

And with the third and final blinding flash Bartholomew turned back into the blond guy he used to be.

'What?!' yelled Gertrude.

'Ask the witch. Let's get out of here,' said Bartholomew.

As you'd expect, they both lived happily ever after. Well, until Bartholomew forgot Gertrude's birthday, and then there was trouble, but that's another story.

The End

Sunshine

I was inspired by stories I have heard my grandfather tell me about his life. He was a Holocaust survivor and the main character in my fairytale is based on him. He escaped from World War II in Poland, hid in Siberia as an adolescent and was separated from his family. Unfortunately, his tale was not as happy as that of my character, he lost his parents and several siblings, but reunited with a few of his siblings in Australia. But, through my grandfather, I have been inspired to believe in hope, courage, determination and the importance of family.

I would like to dedicate my fairytale to my grandfather who has always been the Sunshine in our lives.

Michael, age 11

Once upon a time, in a land far away, there lived an old man called Ethan Waltrop. He was very unhappy and lonely. He spent his time going from house to house, looking for his family that he had lost during a bad war. The tale goes like this.

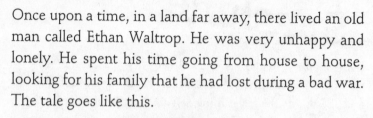

When he was a young boy, a mean ruler from a big city nearby declared war on his little country. Ethan, his parents, his four brothers and three sisters all fled to the hills and tried to hide in them for safety. But a big wind blew so hard that his family separated and were thrown apart. It rained and rained for fifteen weeks and he hid in a dark cave. He lived on very little, just scraps he found of vegetables and plants.

Finally, the sun came out and the land was dry. He walked out and saw a big, bright rainbow and made a wish. He said to himself, 'I wish for a country filled with only love and no more war.' Then he headed to the top of the mountain and looked down, but couldn't find his home or see his family. He cried and cried. In fact he cried so much that a pond of water formed beneath him. Suddenly, a little bird came and drank up all his tears. That bird became his friend and the boy called him **Sunshine**.

Sunshine sat on his shoulder and walked with him in search of his family. He didn't realise at the time, but Sunshine was a special bird that could do magic. If Ethan made a wish, Sunshine fluttered his wings three times and the wish came true. But Ethan didn't realise it, and was very sad, hungry and cold.

He went to sleep on a log and in his dream he uttered the words, 'If only I could be warm.' When he woke, there was a fire burning and his toes were as warm as toast. He thought a miracle must have happened. He turned to Sunshine and said, 'What I would give for some porridge.' Sunshine fluttered his wings and warm, sweet and tasty porridge appeared. He ate and ate 'til his tummy could not fit in another drop. Then he said, 'Sunshine, this is amazing! If only I could be in a lovely warm cottage.' Sunshine fluttered his wings and Ethan found himself sitting in a beautiful cottage filled with everything a young boy could wish for.

Ethan realised he didn't have his family. He said, 'Sunshine, you have brought me food, warmth and comfort. Can you bring back my family?' Sunshine tried. He fluttered and fluttered his wings 'til they ached, but no family appeared. Sunshine tweeted a sad tune and Ethan understood him. Sunshine said, '**Magic works for many things, like toys, food and new homes. But families are so special that you can never recreate them once they are lost**.' Ethan fell in a heap and cried bitterly. Sunshine tweeted, 'I cannot bring you the happiness you desire.' He flew away, sadly.

* * ✳ * *

For many years, Ethan searched from door to door looking for the family he had not seen since that cruel war. He spent his days searching and his nights crying. People felt sorry for him, but no one could replace his family, so he distanced himself from them all. He felt his life had no meaning and there was always a hole that ached in his heart. It was a very sad existence that you would never even wish on your worst enemy.

One day he fell asleep and had a **deep, deep sleep**. In his dream he saw his mother with her golden hair, his dad with a long grey beard, his pretty sisters, kind brothers and their children, all sitting down to dinner. He saw they lived in a land filled with snow, and their house appeared to be at the bottom of a hill.

The next day Ethan set sail on a long journey to every country where it snowed and unsuccessfully searched them one by one. Finally, he travelled by sea to the largest and furthest away island in the world. He saw stunning palaces, and felt like he had been there before, perhaps in his dream.

He again went from door to door with some hope in his steps. He asked everyone in the main town if they had heard of a family called Waltrop. Unfortunately, they all said, 'No.' Each time he heard those words his heart ached more and more.

He wearily travelled down a long, long, narrow road through a remote village. The road seemed to go on forever and his legs ached. He thought about giving up his journey and surrendering to a miserable empty life without his family. Suddenly, his eyes could not believe what they saw. He opened them wide in disbelief and saw the same house he had dreamt of with the shuttered windows and the two chimneys. He knocked on the door and his mother answered.

She exclaimed, 'Ethan, my long lost son, my love, my life. I didn't think you lived through the war and I had thought you couldn't possibly still be alive. You are a dream come true. Our family is complete once more.' These were the words he had hoped to hear for many years.

He sat down at the table and became reacquainted with his brothers and sisters and their children. He found out that the family was blown by the wind into a large vessel travelling to the island. They felt that they were being guided by the moon and the stars. When they arrived, they tried to find a house and a village as close to the one they had left behind as possible.

Ethan told them his story about Sunshine. They couldn't believe that such a lucky, magic bird saved their brother's life. 'If only we could find him and thank him,' the children said. At that moment, Ethan heard a sweet melody outside the window so he opened it. Sunshine flew in and landed on his shoulder.

Sunshine wisely said, 'Only you could find your family, and no magic in the world was enough. Just the love in your heart.'

They all lived happily ever after.

The End

Lord Brazzal of Sprat & his Onion & Potato

The inspiration for 'Lord Brazzal of Sprat and his Onion & Potato' was mainly from my pet mice, Coco and Milo, which my brother Morgan and I received for Christmas 2004. My mouse Milo is Onion in the story. The other part of the inspiration was food.

On Christmas morning, after we opened our presents and had breakfast, Mum told us to go to the bathroom and brush our teeth. We saw Milo and Coco in their cage (a.k.a. a fish tank)—it was a great surprise to see them—we were bugging Mum for about a year to buy mice.

In order to keep the mice a surprise for Christmas morning, they stayed in my Nana's laundry for one week–she was so scared that they would escape and be lost in her house!

Lewis, age 11

This story starts in a castle in Sprat, in the Kingdom of Oobergoff, a land of mystical forests, home of the giant omelette frogs (which, by the way, make delicious omelettes), crystal clear rivers where jumping crouts swim (a close fish relative to the trout), as well as man-eating caves.

The lord of this castle is Lord Brazzal of Sprat. Lord Brazzal is short, stout, very old, and has a face that looks like it's smiling even when it's not. One stormy night, Lord Brazzal of Sprat was running and puffing all the way back to his castle from a meeting of 'Who to Conquer Next'. Lord Brazzal stumbled, almost fell upon, and almost squashed two orphaned baby mice whose mother was mistakenly thought to be a frog and caught and cooked up in an omelette.

Lord Brazzal secretly loved mice. Not even his dear wife, Lady Turnipia of Sprat, knew of Lord Brazzal's love for these cute furry little creatures.

Lord Brazzal knelt down on the damp green grass and scooped up the little sable-coloured mouse and put her in his left pocket. He then picked up the soft grey-spotted mouse and put him in the same pocket so that they were not lonely or scared on the way home. Lord Brazzal of Sprat could feel the mice walking around his left pocket and was smirking to himself all the way home as he was thinking of suitable names. Finally, when he arrived home, with a healthy appetite, he took the mice out of his pocket. The sable mouse he called Potato and the soft grey-coloured mouse he decided to call Onion as these both are delicious ingredients in his favourite food—

omelettes. This made him laugh again and he thought he had better not put them near the kitchen for fear that the cook would mistake them for frogs and put them in an omelette—a dish famous throughout all of Sprat.

Lord Brazzal of Sprat decided that Potato and Onion's house would be in an old, unused drawer in a dressing table used by Lady Turnipia. Lord Brazzal then went to the kitchen and asked the cook to whip up his second favourite dish, crout and brussels sprout soufflé, which he received in fifteen minutes, whisked to his room, and fed to a hungry Onion and Potato. He found Lady Turnipia's sewing basket, and took her only two thimbles, carefully filling them with water and placing them in the drawer with the soufflé. **Onion and Potato loved their new owner very much.**

Every day Lord Brazzal of Sprat would steal himself away from his lordly duties, walk briskly (always puffing), to his room, where he would feed Onion and Potato some soufflé, hold them and gently whisper into their tiny mouse ears how happy they made him. Lord Brazzal and Lady Turnipia were not able to have children of their own.

* * ✳ * *

One sunny afternoon, Lord Brazzal of Sprat was called to a 'Who to Conquer Next' meeting, somewhere in Whakky-doo, a small village next to Whakky-don't. He told Onion and Potato where he was to be going, left them some more soufflé and filled their water thimbles, then he kissed them goodbye.

Without washing his face, he also kissed Lady Turnipia goodbye.

Later that afternoon, back at the castle, Lady Turnipia was madly looking through her sewing basket for a thimble: both seemed to be missing. She was also very confused about the constant smell of crout and brussels sprout soufflé that seemed to always be in their bedroom! Lady Turnipia started opening cupboards and drawers searching for her thimbles—she was getting closer to the drawer where Potato and Onion lived. Lady Turnipia opened the drawer and screamed with fright, turning purple as a turnip, as well as becoming turnip-shaped—not being much different from her usual shape. Onion and Potato could not believe their ears or eyes. In front of them stood **a screaming purple turnip**. Onion and Potato put their cute little paws up to their ears to block the noise and started to cry. This melted Lady Turnipia's heart; she scooped the mice up, instantly feeling a mother's love towards them.

Onion and Potato then proceeded to introduce themselves to Lady Turnipia, who was now fading back to her normal colour, which the mice realised was not as flattering as deep purple. Onion and Potato discussed the now very late time, and the worry they had that Lord Brazzal should have been back from the meeting of 'Who to Conquer Next' by now. Lady Turnipia sent the two mice to find Lord Brazzal, as she also feared he may be in some danger.

Onion and Potato travelled the path Lord Brazzal had travelled earlier that day, encountering masses of giant omelette frogs along the way, crossing crystal clear rivers full of crout, as well as travelling past man-eating caves. They saw a sign pointing to Whakky-doo, which is up a large mountain. Lord Brazzal of Sprat was too unfit to climb the mountain, so he had foolishly taken a shortcut through a cave, forgetting that most of the caves in the Kingdom of Oobergoff are man-eating caves. Luckily he had not been totally devoured by the cave. He was stuck between the large stalagmites and stalactites, also known as teeth.

Onion and Potato quickly found him and slipped inside the man-eating cave. They knew they were safe, as these caves have never been known to eat mice. They tickled the tonsils of the cave, which made it gag and cough Lord Brazzal, Onion and Potato all the way back to the castle of Sprat, where Lady Turnipia was so happy to see Lord Brazzal and her new family safe and sound. The four of them lived happily ever after in a castle in Sprat in the Kingdom of Oobergoff.

The End

A Fruity Fairytale

What inspired me to write 'A Fruity Fairytale' is the fact that I love fruit. Ever since I can remember I have been chomping away at apples or oranges too big for my stomach. I can never resist biting into a juicy piece of watermelon, pineapple or plum because they make my mouth literally water. Imagine life without fruit!

The main dish in the story is an Apple Danish because it relates to the two people I would have loved to meet, Princess Mary, who grew up in The Apple Isle (Tasmania) and Prince Frederik, who is Danish!

Breanna, age 12

Once upon a time, in the kingdom of Frugt Salat, there lived the handsome Fruit Prince. This Prince was widely known throughout the kingdom for his love of fruit. Day after day, the Prince would wander through the acres of the Royal Orchard. Apples, lychees, dragon fruit, mangoes and apricots blossomed all over the trees like Christmas decorations. The **scrumptious** fruit smelt so pure and delicious that one could hardly resist biting into a juicy piece of heaven.

Although the Royal Orchard was everything the Prince had ever wanted, he was extremely lonely and longed for some company. The problem was, the Prince didn't know how to share. He could never bring himself to share his special fruit with anyone. His law stated that only he could eat the juicy fruit of the kingdom. It was for this reason that the Prince remained quite friendless.

The people of Frugt Salat were tired of having such a selfish ruler, so they organised a special meeting in the Town Hall.

'Something's got to be done!' exclaimed the Mayor. 'We can't have the Prince keeping all the kingdom's fruit for himself.'

'That's right,' said the dentist. 'I can't keep on filling everyone's cavities. We need apples and oranges for vitamin C to keep our teeth healthy and strong.'

'What we need is a plan!' called out the local investigator.

'Someone smart who can trick the Fruit Prince,' instructed the teacher.

'OK, who will teach the Fruit Prince a lesson?' asked the Mayor.

Silence fell upon the hall.

'I will,' grunted a voice from the back of the crowd.

Everyone turned around to see a very small, wise man with mysterious green eyes and thin grey hair.

'Very well, then,' said the Mayor, clearing his throat. 'You ought to get cracking if you want your plan to be ready for the Prince's birthday.'

With that, the funny old man disappeared in a puff of smoke.

* * ✳ * *

A week later, the Fruit Prince's birthday had arrived. The cooks were working hard preparing the Fruit Prince's favourite dish, **Apple Danish**, and the Prince was opening his mountain of presents when there was a sharp knock on the door. In came the old, mysterious man looking wiser than ever.

'Who are you and what are you doing here?' declared the Fruit Prince.

'I have come to give you a birthday present, Your Highness. I have brought you a plate.'

'Just a plate?' spat the Prince, looking disgusted.

'Oh, no, Your Highness, this is no ordinary plate. This is a magic plate,' the small man exclaimed, handing it over.

As the Prince looked closer, he could see lots of tiny fruit engraved around the edge of the plate, painted with exotic oranges, greens and yellows.

'It does look beautiful, but ... what does it **do**?'

'This plate will provide you with your **one true desire**. I presume this is the perfect Princess,' the wise old man grinned. 'But you must share all that you have with her or bad things will happen. Don't forget to say "I wish for my perfect Princess".' And the funny old man disappeared in a puff of smoke.

The Prince eagerly but cautiously closed his eyes and said the magic words. Out of the plate came a wisp of smoke that transformed into a frail Princess with long, mousy hair and pale eyes. Her skin was as dry as a sultana.

'Fruit,' she gasped. 'I need fruit!'

The Prince, amazed, hesitantly handed the ugly Princess a plump and juicy mango. The Princess quickly ate it and sighed with relief. She slowly gained colour and transformed into the most beautiful woman the Fruit Prince had ever seen. Her lips were like pink strawberries, and her long curly locks reminded the Prince of grapevine tendrils. Her skin was as smooth as lychee flesh and she smelt like peaches.

The Prince stared dumbstruck at the Princess—it was **love at first sight**.

'Thank you for rescuing me from that magic plate,' she cooed.

'Nnn ... no problem,' the Prince stuttered. 'Ww ... would you like to walk with me in the Royal Orchard?'

'Oh, yes please,' the Princess replied eagerly.

Hand in hand, the Prince and Princess walked through the Royal Orchard until lunchtime. By then, the Prince and Princess were getting hungry so they went back to the palace for the Prince's birthday lunch.

On the table was a banquet of glorious mango curries, chocolate bananas, blueberry muffins and cherry pies. The biggest and most beautiful dish was a sweet Apple Danish, with creamy stewed apple, raspberries and strawberries oozing out of delicate pastry.

Although the Fruit Prince loved the Princess very much, he could not resist the Apple Danish and decided that keeping it for himself could do no harm.

Before the Princess could say, 'Please pass the Apple Danish, dear,' the Prince had scoffed it all down.

Suddenly, the whole kingdom began to shake. Pots and mirrors fell and shattered over the floor. The Prince was terrified and hid under the table, followed by the Princess, who looked very frail.

Before the Prince's eyes, the Princess's skin shrivelled and her beautiful hair turned to powdered ash. The once beautiful Princess was nothing more than a **wrinkly seed.** All of a sudden, the shaking stopped and everything went quiet. The poor Prince stared at the seed and started to sob. He carefully picked up the seed and took it to the Royal Orchard. Not even the irresistible smell of fruit could make the Prince happy.

'I am so sorry, Princess! I will share everything I own with the whole kingdom and never be selfish again. Please forgive me,' the Prince wept.

A tear trickled from the Prince's face and landed on the seed. Slowly but surely a wisp of smoke rose from the seed and transformed into the beautiful Princess once more.

The Prince was delighted. He immediately changed the law so that everyone could eat as much fruit as they desired. The Fruit Prince and Princess walked happily off to share a dish of Apple Danish. Since that day, the sharing kingdom of Frugt Salat has lived happily ever after.

The End

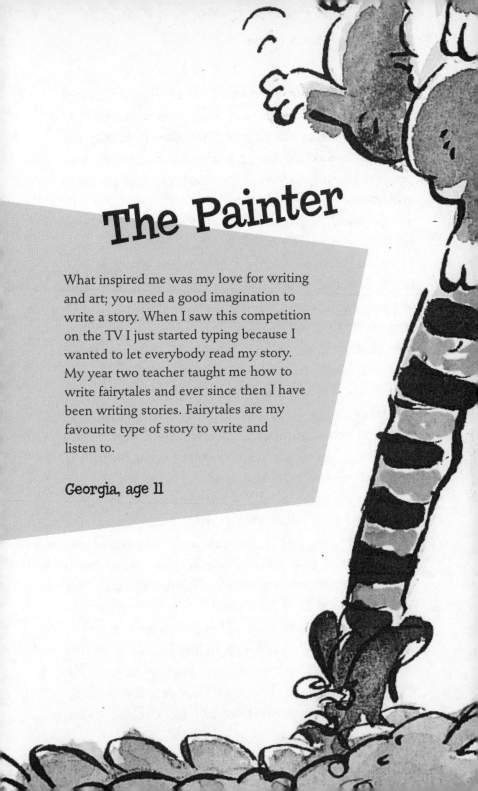

The Painter

What inspired me was my love for writing and art; you need a good imagination to write a story. When I saw this competition on the TV I just started typing because I wanted to let everybody read my story. My year two teacher taught me how to write fairytales and ever since then I have been writing stories. Fairytales are my favourite type of story to write and listen to.

Georgia, age 11

Once upon a time in the land of old England, there was a young girl called Mary who always dreamt of becoming a famous painter. She always hoped her paintings would be hanging on the walls of famous people's houses, maybe in the royal courts of the kings and queens.

She was living with her Uncle Robert, who was the most famous painter in the whole of England, because her father and mother had died when she was very small. She always asked her uncle for lessons on how to paint but Robert thought that women should not be famous for their job or talent, but famous for who they wed and for their beauty. But Mary knew she could be much more than a housewife. She decided to use canvases and paint from her uncle's study.

Her paintings were so realistic and there was always a story in every painting. In the middle of the day, when her uncle went to the country, Mary went out to the street to sell her paintings. Unfortunately she did not get any money because the people who could afford the paintings thought that buying paintings off the street made you look lower class and the other people just could not afford them. She always had to hurry home before her uncle got back. One day her uncle got home early, and he walked into her room while she was putting away the paintings in her hiding spot.

He yelled, 'What are you hiding from me, young lady?' So she had to show the paintings to him. He thought to himself, 'These are wonderful paintings,' and he took them away from her and decided to sell them as his own, without telling Mary.

Three weeks later, Robert had an exhibition of his paintings. Mary loved going to her uncle's exhibitions. She walked in and saw that everyone was crowding around something. She went to have a look. She got through the crowd and there was her painting. Underneath on the left-hand side there was a black line that covered her signature and on the other side was her Uncle Robert's name. She was shocked, and ran outside crying. She sat down and cried and cried, then she realised that one of her tears turned into a bubble. The bubble just got bigger and bigger, and when it popped, out fell a fairy.

The fairy said, 'What's the matter, child?'

Mary said, 'My uncle took my paintings and sold them as his own.'

Shocked, the fairy said, 'Why, that's awful. Now, to bigger matters: what is your name, child?'

Mary replied, 'My name is Mary Elisabeth Taylor, but just call me Mary. Who are you?'

'Well, I'm your fairy godmother and I'm here to wish all your worries away. All I need is for you to wish for something and I will grant your wish.'

Mary closed her eyes and started wishing. Her wish was that her uncle would be punished for selling her paintings as his. That moment inside the hall, the Mayor scratched off the black line and there was Mary's name. The Mayor was furious; he could now see what Mary's uncle had done. Mary's name was clear on the painting. The Mayor decided to banish the uncle from his town for the remainder of his life, and to give Mary a chance to fulfil her dreams. Mary cried out to her fairy godmother, 'Oh, fairy godmother, oh, fairy godmother.' She was gone.

The next day Mary moved out of her uncle's house and moved into her new house with a studio that was just for her. She bought canvases and paint, fulfilling her lifelong dream.

The End

Scorchio the Dragon

The main thing that inspired my story, 'Scorchio The Dragon', was my love of spaghetti and the tomato sauce my mum makes that goes on it. It is yummy! I also like dragons. When I wrote the story I had just been given a beautiful book on dragons to read.

I've also always wanted to be a princess! I think I would make a good one and if I was a princess I would want to live in a royal palace, with my own pet dragon.

Rebecca, age 7

Once upon a time there lived a King who loved his spaghetti, even though it was never hot enough because the Royal Stove didn't work properly. Even more than his spaghetti, the King loved his tomato sauce that went with it. In the Royal Garden the King grew beautiful tomatoes for the Royal Kitchen. Every morning he polished the tomatoes with a special cloth he kept in a treasure chest because he really liked to have clean tomatoes.

Unknown to the King, nearby lived a fire-breathing dragon named Scorchio. He was beautiful because he had bright colours all over him. Scorchio was friends with the Royal Princess, Becky. They played together. They loved having campfires and eating marshmallows that Scorchio would cook for them.

One day Scorchio decided to have a tiny peek at the Royal Palace and he accidentally coughed on the King's Royal Garden and it went up in flames.

The Princess gave Scorchio some money to buy some tomatoes to make up to the King for the burnt garden. Scorchio went to the supermarket but when he got there, no one would serve him because everyone was scared, even though he was only a tiny dragon and wouldn't hurt anyone, so he put the coins on the counter and took the tomatoes.

Scorchio went with Princess Becky to the palace to give them to the King, but they couldn't find the King because he was crying in his garden. Princess Becky and Scorchio went to the Royal Kitchen to give the tomatoes to the Royal Chef, who was trying to boil some water for the Royal Spaghetti. Scorchio accidentally coughed on the saucepan of water on the stove and the saucepan water boiled. The Royal Chef asked if Scorchio, to make up for the burnt Royal Garden, would come every day and boil the water for the Royal Spaghetti.

And then Scorchio played with everyone in the Royal Palace because everyone realised he was a nice dragon. They gave him free marshmallows and he always shared them with the Princess. And they all lived happily ever after.

The End

Princess Plum's Prophecy

Ever since a very young age I dreamt of becoming a princess. You would often find me skipping around the supermarket with my mum, wearing a pink, fluffy tiara. But as I grew older I began to think more about this dream ...

Maybe becoming a princess might not be so great after all. You would probably have to live a fairly restricted life, trying to live up to everyone else's expectations; the pressure would be enormous!

As I realised this, Princess Plum's Prophecy was born.

Amy, age 12

Once upon a time, twin princesses were born. The King and Queen were overjoyed and named them Princess Peach and Princess Plum.

As everyone knows, all royal children need to have a prophecy made for them on their seventh birthday. When the time came, the King called in the Limerick Bunyip (who was a bit dotty) to cast a prediction over the girls.

This is what he said for Princess Peach:

You are a very nice child,
And I think your luck will be piled.
You'll find true love,
From up above,
And your house will be splendidly tiled.

Next he turned to Princess Plum. He thought for a very long time before he spoke:

Although you may look nice,
I think people should think twice.
Your favourite fella,
Should buy an umbrella,
And you'll love making coconut ice.

Then, with a mysterious swiff of the Limerick Bunyip's paw, a dark cloud appeared over Princess Plum's head. In the next moment he was gone.

Furious at the strange prophecy the King glared at Princess Plum and shouted, 'I cannot be known as the father of this **MISTAKE!**'

Princess Plum's lips began to tremble, her whole body began to shake and she erupted into tears. Above her head, the rain cloud did likewise and rained down on her.

'Princess Plum,' the Queen shouted. 'You are a **freak!**'

'She's right,' the King snarled. 'You are nothing but a frowzy, frumpish, freak of nature! Look at that ridiculous rain cloud hanging above your head. I can't put up with this nonsense! Go and live in the cottage in the back of the palm plantation. **GET OUT!**'

Princess Plum ran sobbing and spluttering out to the cottage (which was just as well because she was flooding the palace).

* * ✳ ✳ *

As time passed, it seemed that everybody forgot about Princess Plum. Every day she gazed through the cottage window, and every night she kept herself busy mopping up her tears and the sad rain that fell from her cloud.

On her nineteenth birthday, she saw her sister weaving her way up through the coconut palms towards the cottage. She was holding a beautiful cake and Princess Plum imagined that on top was written, **'I'm sorry for not visiting you in the last twelve years. Happy birthday!'**

By the time Princess Peach was about fifteen metres away, Princess Plum was imagining how good the cake would taste and how wonderful it would be to reunite with her sister. Then something shocking happened ...

One of the King's coconut collectors fell out of the tree right above Princess Peach. Princess Peach held up the cake to shield herself. It was a bad sight as nineteen burning candles collided with the coconut collector's face.

Although the burns were horrific and the cream was non-dairy, the pair looked at each other and it was clear, even to Princess Plum, that it was love at first sight for Princess Peach and the coconut collector. The couple turned and walked back to the palace hand in hand, having found true love.

The next week, Princess Plum could hear the wedding bells and she cried so much she flooded the cottage. Her **tears** and **rain** overflowed into the surrounding garden. She continued to cry for the next six months.

During this time a drought had taken hold of the kingdom. All over the land people were starving and everything was dull and lifeless. Everywhere, that is, except for the garden around Princess Plum's cottage which, thanks to her continuous tears and rain, was lush and green with fruit trees and lots of tropical plants. It was a bright blur of colour and a joy to look at compared to the colourless surroundings.

After a while, the gardener boy began to notice the loveliness around the cottage and decided to investigate. It was a very good thing he did because, as fate would have it, Princess Plum and the gardener boy were a perfect match. Immediately, they embraced. Plum felt so happy in the gardener boy's caring arms that the big dark rain cloud above her head turned into a fluffy white cloud.

Gently, the gardener boy took Princess Plum's hand and let her out of the cottage for the first time in twelve years, six months and one week. Together they walked all over the drought-stricken kingdom and the sorrow that Princess Plum saw in the people's faces made her cry all over again. Rain poured out of the cloud above her head as she sobbed and sobbed.

Everywhere that Princess Plum and the gardener walked, green plants grew up in their wake. By the time they returned to the cottage, the whole kingdom was lusciously green and everyone rejoiced. The following week they got married.

Just as Princess Plum said 'I do,' the minister transformed into the Limerick Bunyip and with a mysterious swiff of his paw, the cloud above Princess Plum's head disappeared and a beautiful rainbow emerged over everybody's head.

The sisters set up business next to each other: Princess Peach's Tile Emporium and Princess Plum's Coconut Treats. The gardener boy and the coconut collector went into business making umbrellas.

And they all lived happily ever after.

The End

The Very Plain Egg

The reason I wrote 'The Very Plain Egg' was because I heard a story at church one Sunday. It was about honesty and persistence. I had heard about the fairytale competition earlier that morning, but I had no ideas about what to write then. The story that I heard at church gave me a fantastic theme that I could use in an interesting way. I love writing stories and I hope you enjoy this one.

Yours sincerely,

Jade, age 8

Once upon a time, in a kingdom far away, there lived a King who was growing very old. As the bright autumn leaves fell from the trees, he decreed that all the kingdom's children must come to the castle.

'I have decided that one of you children shall be the next king or queen,' he declared.

The children whispered frantically, wondering who the King would choose.

'You will each be given **an egg**,' the King continued. 'But you must hatch this egg, feed the animal and, above all, love it. In one year's time, the child who has done the best job will be crowned as ruler.'

Beside the King there was a huge basket of eggs and all the children rushed forward.

'Out of the way, pipsqueak! Surely you didn't think the King meant to include you,' said the bigger kids, shoving one poor orphan girl to the ground. She was indeed small and underfed, but she picked herself up and wiped tears from her blue eyes and joined the end of the line. All the eggs were dyed a different colour of the rainbow. Some were blue, some red, some yellow like gold and some as silver as the moon. When Joy, the little orphan girl, finally reached the basket, there was one last egg left. It was small, with a little crack in the dirty white shell, but she still took it, cradling it in her little hands to keep it warm.

Joy looked after that egg all autumn. She had no family and she lived in a tiny room at the back of the village tailor's shop and did the chores like fetching the water from the stream, sweeping out the shop, and running errands. Every day she had to work very hard and never had any time to play, but she always checked on her egg every morning and evening and wrapped it in a scarf made from scraps of cloth. Winter arrived and other children sometimes came into the shop with their new pets. Primrose, the daughter of the pompous Mayor, was always acting like a princess. Her egg hatched into a beautiful peacock.

She saw Joy sweeping the floor and said, 'See what my egg hatched out as. The King will have to pick me. What was in your sad little egg?'

Joy did not reply and went to get the dustpan and shovel.

The jeweller's son, Jet, came in for new boots. He had black hair, dark eyes and a nasty temper. A beautiful golden dragon was coiled across his shoulders. Megan, the toyshop-keeper's daughter, also arrived. Her animal was a chameleon and it was bright orange to match the colour of the beautiful new dress her mother had bought after one of Megan's many tantrums.

'Look how beautiful my pet is. I'm sure to win. I hear that some people haven't even managed to hatch out anything at all,' she said, looking at Joy.

'Not even a chicken,' sneered Jet.

By winter's end, Joy's egg still had not hatched but she kept tending it. She was sent on an errand to the baker for a loaf of bread. The baker's boy, Phillip, was always kind to her and often gave her yesterday's crusts if no one was looking. He told her that his egg had not hatched yet either and not to give up.

Joy's egg hatched in the second week of spring. She thought that it was **the strangest creature** she had ever seen. It had the bill and the feet of a duck, the tail of a beaver and a small spike on its left foot. It was covered in coarse brown fur and looked up at her with bright brown eyes full of mischief. Joy named it Wade, and kept it in her apron pocket, fed it scraps and let it play by the stream whenever she went to fetch water. On the way back one day she met Madison, who was always bossy, greedy and rude. Upon seeing Joy's strange little bundle she said, 'That is the most ridiculous thing I have ever seen.'

In summer, Joy taught Wade how to catch shrimp at the stream where the other children sometimes came to play.

Primrose said, '**Eww**. What is that ugly thing?'

Jet said, 'At first I did not believe Madison when she said what a ridiculous thing you had hatched.'

Even Phillip, the baker's boy, was mean. His egg had finally hatched and he had a snake, with glittering silver scales, twined round his arm. 'My egg took a long time to hatch but at least it was worth the wait,' he said and ran off along the riverbank with the other children.

* * ✳ * *

Autumn came again with chill winds and a shower of leaves. The King called all the children back to the palace. They lined up in the courtyard while he observed them. Joy felt very nervous and scared, but at least she was at the back of the line. The King looked at each of the many beautiful creatures that the children had brought, including the golden dragon, the regal peacock, the silver snake and a bright rainbow lorikeet. Finally the King came to Joy.

'What is your name?'

'Joy, Your Majesty,' she said.

'Step up to the front,' ordered the King. 'Children, this is our new ruler.'

'What?' Joy was gobsmacked.

'But how?' cried all the children. 'She is just a grubby little orphan girl. All our pets are far more beautiful.'

The King said, 'You all got platypus eggs and when your eggs did not hatch quickly enough, or when you did not like what you got, you replaced them. Joy was the only one who didn't, and she loved and nurtured her egg right from the first time she saw it. It has given her the right to be the next Queen.'

'But can I still keep Wade?' Joy said.

'Of course,' replied the King.

Joy grew up to be a kind and generous Queen and they all lived happily ever after, even those who had not learned that persistence and honesty lead to success.

The End

Rose

Fairytales have been a part of my life ever since I can remember. I heard about Hans Christian Andersen's 'The Wild Swans' from my parents in the warmth of our home in the Himalayan Kingdom of Bhutan, where I spent most of my earlier childhood years. Later, on our small property in Victoria, reading about the intriguing personalities in George MacDonald's fantasies, J.R.R. Tolkien's Middle Earth and C.S. Lewis's Narnia world inspired me.

It seemed like part of that fairytale world when Mary Donaldson married Crown Prince Frederik.

I have five younger brothers and sisters, and it was my six-year-old sister, Jemimah, who thought of the plot for 'Rose', suggesting I write a tale about a 'princess who is turned into a rose'. I followed her suggestion, this being the result. Along with J.R.R. Tolkien, I believe that fairytales ought to have a happy ending.

Hannah, age 14

Once upon a time, there was a young girl who was known to her people as Princess Rosamond. People whispered about her beauty as far away as the Eastern Shores, for her hair was said to resemble the radiance of sunshine, her skin the translucency of a moonstone and her lips the sweetness of a cherry. She was the apple of her father's eye.

There happened to be a wicked witch who was not at all fond of either the Princess or her father. The reason for this was the King had banished her and others of her kind from the land, though many of them still lived there in secret. While left sulking in a large, dark castle the witch plotted her **evil plan**.

One day, when small white clouds played in the blue dome that covered the palace, the Princess felt herself drawn to the beauty of the outside realm. Summer breezes tossed her golden hair as she moved through the palace garden. Sitting upon an old wooden bench she watched a family of wrens dancing and hopping. Her head nodded against the wooden railings as drowsiness overtook her, quite unaware that she was being observed. The witch's hand flew in the air, scattering a flurry of shimmering rose petals, filling the air and covering the Princess. Rosamond's form disappeared, leaving only the scented petals and the hopping wrens.

The King did not know what to make of his daughter's disappearance and a seat covered with rose petals. The entire palace searched for a month, seeking their beloved Princess throughout the kingdom. The King, refusing to believe his daughter was irretrievable, sent forth a proclamation declaring that '**whoever finds the Princess shall inherit half the kingdom**'. Accordingly, the palace was soon overrun with eager young men trying to find their fortune.

* * ✳ * *

There happened to be a nobleman whose son had just arrived home. After hearing of the Princess's disappearance, he was determined to get to the bottom of the matter. He approached his father to determine his course of action. His father explained that bitterness often runs against those in power. He told his son to find out if anything the King had done would have caused offence to any person.

James Balfore (for that was his name) found his search for information fruitful. He learned of the witches' banishment and anger against the King. Was it not likely that a witch had spirited the Princess away? He found out that those of the witches that had disappeared had run to the Dark Forest in the North, where they had allied themselves with phantoms and other such evil beings that lived there.

At dawn a few days later a rider with a sword by his side could be seen on a white stallion riding north.

James Balfore came to the Dark Forest sometime before nightfall. It was a formidable sight, the dark overhanging branches intertwined with mistletoe that seemed to speak of great evil. James's horse needed much encouragement before entering the small, winding path that led through the trees. The forest seemed horribly dark and deserted. The gaps between the leaves far overhead warned of the coming of rain.

Suddenly his horse bolted, and James saw the reason for his horse's fright. **A face, pale and lifeless, with blue lips and empty eyes stared at him**, a face framed by long black hair that streamed out in a most startling manner. The stallion ran, the phantom moving fast alongside them. The horse worked itself into a frenzy and charged into the undergrowth, which, much to James's surprise, brought them out of the dreaded forest. He saw a barren wasteland that stretched out as far as the eye could see. To the right of him, a large, grey stone castle stood, foreboding against the dark sky.

* * ✳ * *

It so happened that all the witches were attending a huge gathering, thrown by the chief witch. None of them suspected that a visitor would appear.

James Balfore galloped up to the gates. The large wooden gates were shut tight. James looked around to see if there was any other entrance. He noticed a curious thing when he glanced around. **A single rose grew on a bush** below a turret. Its brightness was stark against the colourless backdrop.

James saw that the only way to enter the castle was by climbing in a window in the turret. Fashioning his rope into a lasso, he swung it to a gargoyle that jutted from the roof and hoisted himself up, leaving his horse below. By this time, the witches had heard of his arrival and rushed to the turret. When James entered the small room, he was confronted by screaming women.

'Where is Princess Rosamond?' asked James, drawing his sword.

The witches, however, paid no heed to his words. 'Back to where you came from, dog!' they shrieked.

James had not been prepared for so many hysterical witches in high dudgeon against him. He was therefore not ready when he was hauled up and thrust out the window, the shrieks of the witches still ringing in his ears. He was falling. He did not despair, for he saw that the rose bush was going to cushion his fall. The bush broke under his weight, causing the single rose to fall.

The witches shrieked. A flurry of shimmering rose petals filled the air, covering the rose. And it seemed to James Balfore that the rose had turned into a girl of great beauty, whose **hair resembled sunshine, her skin a moonstone and her lips the sweetness of a cherry**.

'Are you my rescuer?' asked the Princess, somewhat dazed.

'Yes, and you mine, My Lady. Hurry, follow me!'

Seizing her hand, he pulled her to his horse and placed her on the saddle. With the shrieks and curses of the witches following them, they raced into the Dark Forest. They caught only a glimpse of a pale face and empty eyes, for they were out of the forest speedily.

On their arrival, the King threw his arms about his daughter and kissed her. However, when he heard about James's encounter with the phantoms and witches, he was shocked. He immediately called his brigade to clean out the Dark Forest. When it was no longer haunted by evil things, it became quite pleasant, and the old grey castle was turned into a summer retreat for the King, who grew roses all around it. When James and the Princess married, they spent their honeymoon there.

As James was entitled to half the kingdom for rescuing Rosamond, and Rosamond owned the other half, it remained their beloved land, where everyone lived happily ever after.

The End

Heroes in Disguise

I was inspired to write my fairytale by a few things. One was Andy Griffiths the author, who writes hilarious books for young people and they are full of crazy and funny incidents. Also my English teacher, who has been encouraging me to go another step with my story telling. And because I was so bored out of my brains one day, Mum sent me to my room so I wrote a story. And if it wasn't for my loving parents pushing me to enter, I wouldn't have done it, so thanks to you all. Love ya!

Chantelle, age 14

In a small town called Fidgety, there lived a family called **Rickety Pickety**. Roger Rickety Pickety, the father, was a quiet and very simple man. He never said much unless it was necessary. Fran Rickety Pickety, the mother, was always trying hard to make the family fit in. She would get so down and depressed if things went wrong. These two parents were blessed with three quite peculiar children.

Paige, their eldest daughter, aged fifteen, was fascinated by maggot guts. Wherever there was a massacre of dead flies, there was Paige poking around like a vulture at a dead body. Their son, Timmy, aged ten, absolutely loved brussels sprouts. He had them for breakfast, lunch and tea. He would eat them by the mouthful. Their youngest daughter, Cinnamon, aged ten months, did not like anyone, not even her parents. Whenever someone tried to pick her up from the cot, she would yell and scream and start to scratch.

The Rickety Pickety family were known as the Fidgety Town 'freaks'. No matter how hard they tried to be normal, it just didn't work. For example, when the family tried to go for a nice stroll around the block, Paige found a **maggot** lying there on the ground. Being Paige the maggot freak, she rushed straight over to it and started to poke it and squeeze all its insides out. To make it even worse, she ran around in circles screaming her lungs out, 'It's pregnant, it's pregnant!' Not to mention that Cinnamon was crying and screaming the whole way.

People were so scared and ashamed of the Rickety Pickety family that when they saw them, they would either run and hide, or just look at them and shake their heads. This, as it would for anyone, made the Rickety Pickety family extremely depressed.

'Oh, Roger,' Fran would plead. 'When will this town learn to accept the fact that we're just not like other people?'

Roger would always reply, 'Well, Fran, I just don't know.'

The Mayor of the town, Mayor Lukens, was getting sick and tired of people always sending in complaints about the Rickety Pickety family. Some of the letters were just to make the Mayor get so upset that he would send them out of town. One person sent in a letter saying:

Dear Mr Mayor Lukens,

Today I saw the Rickety Pickety family down at the supermarket. Normally I wouldn't care less what other people buy in the shop, but I noticed that Mrs Fran Rickety Pickety was buying an awful lot of brussels sprouts. I also noticed that her daughter Paige was cutting almost every apple in half and while she was doing so she was muttering under her breath which made it sound like she wanted to kill someone with a whole bunch of maggots. And their baby would not stop crying. All this commotion forced me to storm out of the supermarket because I was so frazzled.

This letter got Mayor Lukens so angry that he went and visited the Rickety Pickety family.

'Sadly,' Mayor Lukens began, 'I have had a lot of complaints about your family and I have no choice but to send you out of town.'

'But we can't move,' said Fran Rickety Pickety. 'Just give us a chance!'

'I'm sorry, Fran,' explained Mayor Lukens. 'You have to move; the people in the town have all agreed to let you go.'

'Roger, say something!' Fran yelled.

'Arh, well, I don't know,' said a startled Roger.

'The only way this town will let you back in is if you prove yourself worthy to live here again,' said Mayor Lukens.

So the Rickety Pickety family had no choice but to move. Luckily for them, they didn't have to buy a house because their Aunty Pointy Nose (she really lived up to her name!) had been banished to the same town, the Town of Banishment!

* * ✳ * *

About two weeks later, when the Rickety Pickety family were sitting down to watch the news, they saw an unusual sight.

'Shhhhh,' said Roger.

'Citizens of Fidgety Town have been forced to evacuate. Last Monday, a tragic thing happened ...' All of a sudden, the television screen went blank.

'What is it?' screamed Roger. 'What's the tragic thing?'

'Oh, dear,' said Fran.

So off the Rickety Picketys went to see what this tragic incident was.

* * ✳ * *

When they arrived at Fidgety Town, there they saw a fifty-foot-tall, **pink, green and black snot**.

'Oh, thank goodness you guys are here,' said Mayor Lukens, who was out of breath. 'This snot is out of control and, believe it or not, the only way to kill it is to gross it out. Can you please help us?'

'Roger, this is our chance to prove ourselves worthy to move back,' said Fran.

'Well, what are you waiting for?' said Roger. '**Let's gross this pig out of its brains!**'

'Umm, Dad, it is a snot,' pointed out Paige.

'Oh, whatever, let's get rid of it.'

The Rickety Picketys did the most disgusting and unusual things that any of the townspeople had ever seen. They fired chewed-up brussels sprouts, not to mention the spewed-up ones. They squirted maggot guts at it, screamed in its ears and the rest is so disgusting that it would be illegal to put it in this story.

'Help me! I'm melting into nothing. Slowly fading, fading, fading ... gone!' cried the snot.

'Well, Rickety Picketys, you have proven yourselves more than worthy to stay in this town. We apologise for our rudeness and would like to welcome you back into Fidgety Town,' said Mayor Lukens.

'We are more than happy to be back,' said the Rickety Picketys.

After that, no one ever criticised the Rickety Picketys again.

The End

The Princess Who Was Different

I wanted my Princess to be different from the princesses I have always read about. I thought it would be fun to make her do things like I do on our farm. I wanted her to be modern and a bit of a tomboy as well.

I decided to put the Lithgow Panther into my story as a family joke because my stepdad is always reading and talking about the Lithgow Panther. We always make family jokes when he reads about it on the Internet (and he knows nothing about computers so that makes it even funnier).

Samantha, age 11

Once upon a time there was a beautiful young Princess. The beautiful Princess was called Prudence. She was by far the most beautiful princess in all of Australia and boys (who thought they could pretend they were princes) used to come from afar to look at her standing in her treehouse balcony, flicking spitballs down upon them.

Prudence was not your normal, everyday princess. She liked to go and climb trees, she liked to play cricket, she loved mudwrestling and she really loved riding her motorbike and jumping it high over the big dirt mounds around the palace grounds.

The King and Queen of 'Prudeville' were not happy that Princess Prudence liked to do all of these things and they were always nagging her to be a lady. Princess Prudence would shake her head and say, 'Whatever,' and put her hand up towards them, walking off and muttering under her breath, 'Talk to the hand.'

One day Princess Prudence was way out in the back paddocks (where her mum and dad told her not to go because it was too far away), scaring rabbits out of their holes with her pet ferrets. The ferrets were being naughty and would not come out of the rabbit hole. Princess Prudence was feeling a bit grumpy and did not want to go back to the palace and get the shovel and have to dig them out. She was wondering how to scare them out and was cursing loudly when all of a sudden, ***POOF!!!!***, there was heaps of dust everywhere.

'Blimey jeebies!' said Prudence. 'What the hell are you?'

The funny-looking thing wiped its eyes and looked Prudence up and down. Prudence looked it up and down.

It was big … very big, and also very black. 'Hello,' it said. 'I am the Lithgow Panther.'

'**Bulldust!**' said Prudence. 'Everybody knows that that is just a big load of bulldust!'

'Well, it's not,' said the Panther. 'Here I am. I have been running and running for ages in the Blue Mountains. I come down every now and then to have something to eat, not causing anyone any harm, when "**Eeeeeeee eeeeeeeeeeekkkkkkkkkkkkk,**" someone sees me and starts screaming and running around like a chook with its head cut off.'

'Well, what are you doing in our kingdom?' said Prudence. 'And how did you get here?'

The Panther looked a bit funny and then called Prudence over in a whisper.

'Well, don't tell anyone, but I was stealing a picnic basket out of a hot air balloon when it took off. I was lucky to get out of there with my life! I have been hanging on the bottom of that basket for ages. I am scared of heights, too, I tell you!'

Princess Prudence looked at him doubtfully.

'It's true I tell ya!' the Panther said. 'I couldn't hang on any more and I fell. That is why I landed here and there was all that dust!'

Princess Prudence shook her head. She was thinking to herself about how she would become really famous when she rang the papers and told them about how she found the Lithgow Panther! Her dad, the King, was always on the Internet reading about it—and here, right next to her, she had it!

She scratched her head and thought to herself how she was going to catch him and trap him. All of a sudden she had a light globe above her head (which meant she had a good idea).

Princess Prudence invited the Lithgow Panther back to the palace. She told him she was going to be his good friend and that she would make him a secret house where he would never have to run away and people would never be afraid of him.

This all sounded pretty good to the Lithgow Panther—and he didn't really get much out of that picnic box before the hot air balloon took off.

'Well, come on then, Panther. Jump on the dog box on the back of my motorbike,' said Princess Prudence.

'**Hmmmmmmm**,' said the Lithgow Panther. 'Can you ride it very well?'

'I'm a legend,' said Prudence. 'Just ask me and I'll tell ya.'

The Panther said, 'What about your pet ferrets?'

'Don't worry,' said Prudence. 'I'll just get some new ones.'

The Lithgow Panther climbed onto the dogbox and they sped off.

Princess Prudence rode very fast and took her usual track, which involved going over big bumps that sent them soaring into the sky very high! The Lithgow Panther was clinging to the seat with his claws, hanging on for his dear life.

When they got to the palace, Princess Prudence took the Panther up to her treehouse (he got up there because cats can climb). The Panther quickly locked the door behind her, pounced on Princess Prudence and gobbled her all up. He then ran off as quickly as he could and lived happily ever after back in the Lithgow region, where he is still famous.

You probably think this is a horrible ending to the story, **don't you?** Well, it was going to be nice 'til the Lithgow Panther saw Prudence leave her pet ferrets behind: that really angered him. Plus, the ride back to the palace on the back of the motorbike really got up his nose. She was not a very nice girl.

The moral of the story is: never leave your ferrets down a rabbit hole and don't talk to strange panthers. Also, you'd better listen to your parents (well, sometimes!).

The End

The Troll's Bride

I was inspired to write this story because I used to tell it as a little girl. It was my favourite bedtime story. I made up all the details of the pretend cakes and dances. Mum and I would even act them out during the story! The grosser the trolls were, the better. I hope other children enjoy it as much as I have.

Molly, age 8

Once upon a time, on a magical island, there lived a King and Queen. They were very happy in their kingdom except for the frequent earthquakes.

Deep under the ground there lived a troll called Tufto. When the troll was upset or angry, his stomping and yelling would cause those terrible upsetting earthquakes. The Queen got so fed up with all her good china being broken that she sent for the royal unicorns.

The Queen had decided the unhappy troll needed a wife. She would hold a competition to find the right one. The unicorns searched the world and brought back three contestants.

The next day they all headed to the Royal Park, where the competition was to be held. The King and Queen sat on royal chairs with Tufto next to them. The Queen stood up and explained the rules.

'The first test will be a singing contest. The second test will be to bake a cake and the final test will be to perform a dance.'

The first troll stood up to perform her song. She had pink hair that curled up into a large ball. Her song sounded like owls hooting and cows mooing. Tufto smiled. The second troll had straight blue hair that fell to the ground. Her voice sounded like a mix of frogs croaking and **trolls burping**. The final troll had black dreadlocks with two white mice living inside. Tufto declared the pink troll the winner of the singing contest.

The trolls began to bake their cakes. The pink troll's ingredients were pink slugs mixed with snail shells, cobwebs and mosquito blood. She iced it with pink paint. The blue troll used blue pen ink, pencil shavings, snot and a touch of rotten apple cores. The dreadlocked troll used mouse fur, mouse droppings, worms and a hint of spit! Tufto said, 'The blue cake is the most scrumdiddlyumptious cake I've ever eaten!!' **(The Queen was very glad she didn't have to eat any of them!)**

The troll band picked up their weird and wonderful instruments and began to play their weird and wonderful music. The trolls moved onto the dance floor and began their moves. They looked very funny.

The pink troll danced like a giant gorilla. The blue troll danced so slowly that people were falling asleep while watching her. The dreadlocked troll danced a troll rap that was so groovy the audience were bopping in their seats. When the dance finished, the Queen turned to Tufto and asked him, 'Who do you choose to be your wife?'

'Well,' said Tufto. 'That is a very hard question to answer. I love listening to beautiful music. I love eating delicious food. However, the thing that truly makes my heart sing with joy is to **DANCE!** I choose the troll with dreadlocks to be my wife.'

From that day on, there has been peace in the kingdom. Some days the Queen's china will rattle a little and she can hear music coming from somewhere. She smiles, knowing that way down below her, there is a great dance party going on at the troll's house.

The End

The Little Doll

My Recipe for Inspiration

* A room full of soft toys, each with a spark
* A special toy, a spotty dog, beginning to bark
* A cotton reel doll, all dressed up in blue
* An broken down sign, fixed up with glue
* An innocent smile
* A pure, freckled face
* Mix it together, with lots of straight trust
* Then add just a pinch of pure fairy dust ...

Simmer for 20 minutes, don't let it grow cold.
Don't let your story go by untold.

Catherine, age 14

Once upon a time in a small village in England, an old man was making his way slowly through the snow to his house above his shop. The old man was hunched over, his cloak billowing behind him in the wind. He could just make out the tattered sign that hung, slightly bent, over the door. The words were obscured and wrecked by vandals who just didn't appreciate things any more. The windows were closed and the house was dark and forbidding. The old man fumbled as he took his keys out of his pocket. With trembling hands, stiff from the cold, he brought them towards the lock. But something stopped him. A rare piece of colour shone out from under the snow. It looked out of place in the dark, dreary street. The old man bent down, and groaned as his joints creaked. He lifted the colour from the snow and saw that it was **a rag doll, lost and forgotten**. Its face was streaked with mud and its dress was torn. The old man gently put her in his pocket and proceeded to open the door. What he didn't see was the small smile which had developed on the little doll's face.

After the old man went to bed that night, the little doll crept out of his pocket. The shop was dark and scary, but the little doll had courage and knew what she had to do. Eyes stared out at her from the darkness, lights in a dark world. These were the eyes of the desperate: the lonely, lost souls of forgotten toys, and filled with memories. The old man had collected them from the streets to try to find their owners and give them back their life. But he was old and getting on in his life. Try as he might, he could not mend these toys. This was the doll's job.

The little doll worked tirelessly throughout the night, the old man gently snoring in the background. One by one the toys came alive. **Their eyes shone** and they felt a warmth like never before. Still the little doll worked. She would not stop until every one of these forgotten souls had been reborn.

Morning came. The workshop was quiet, but there was a warm feeling about it. Gone was the darkness and cold. The old man made his way slowly down the stairs from his room. He could feel something different, but he wasn't sure what. When he reached the bottom of the stairs, his face cracked into a smile, which lit up the room. He hadn't had much to smile about since his wife had died. His smile shone so brightly that people in the streets stopped as they passed by, to look in the now clean windows of the shop. They saw at once what he was smiling about. For there on his bench were all the toys the old man had collected over the years. They were mended and they looked just like new. And on top of the pile was the little rag doll. She looked the same as she had when the old man had picked her up. Her hair was still tousled and her dress was ripped and torn.

Then it happened. A huge crowd had gathered outside the old man's shop. A young boy in the front of the crowd suddenly yelled out, 'Felix!' He ran inside the shop and grabbed one of the teddies the doll had mended.

'Thank you, Mister!' the boy said shyly to the old man and then ran out of the shop.

The old man was astounded. He had thought that

the toys had been forgotten and dumped. One by one more children came in and took their lost toys. This continued until all the toys but one had been claimed. The little doll was left, staring blankly at the ceiling. All of the onlookers had dispersed, until again, all but one was left. A little girl stood in the snow outside the shop. The old man saw her and beckoned her inside.

'Please, Sir, may I have my doll? I lost her a few days ago.'

The old man looked at her and smiled. 'Would you like me to fix her up, mend her hair and darn her dress?'

The little girl looked into the old man's eyes and replied, 'Thank you, but no, Sir. **I think she's perfect already**.'

The old man picked up the little doll and handed her to the girl. 'I agree, she is one special doll.'

And he could have sworn that the little doll had winked.

The End

A True Fairy Tail

My friend Chanel and I were talking about fairytales because our class was making fairytale puppets. I said, 'None of these fairytales are really true because none of the fairies in them have TAILS.' We both started laughing.

I told my mum about this and she said it would be good to write a fairytale about a fairy with a tail.

The Thistle Queen, the bad character in my story, came to me when I was walking our dog down the creek where there are lots of tall thistles. I thought they'd make a good bad character.

Miranda, age 10

Once upon a time there was a very beautiful fairy named Cordelia. She lived in a plum tree with her grandma and they earned their living by making plum jam.

Wait, I started this story wrong because Cordelia wasn't just a fairy, she was a fairy with a tail. Cordelia often wondered about fairytales. She was a bit confused because absolutely no one in them had tails, so why were they called 'fairy tails'?

Anyway, one day Cordelia and her grandma were at the markets selling jam, but no one wanted to buy jam. Cordelia wandered up to the stall next door. It was a newspaper stall. Cordelia picked up a newspaper. It read:

The Thistle Queen has escaped from jail. If you find her, bring her to Fairy Headquarters and you will receive a reward of 100 gold coins and a secret. She has returned to her palace and is making more thistles by the second. Beware of the traps she has set.

As soon as Cordelia read this she planned her journey. She knew where the Thistle Queen lived and it wasn't very far away. She set off and after a while she came to the Thistle Queen's house ... or, where she thought it was. But there was only an open field.

By this time, Cordelia was getting tired so she lay down to have a rest. When she lay down she noticed that she could see some thistles. She knew what was going on. It was a wall of invisibility. There was a crack, and through it, Cordelia could see the Thistle Queen's palace. She got up and flew over the wall. Now she could see the palace really well. But wait, she saw a blue-tongue lizard. It looked hurt. She went down to the ground to help it, but as soon as she landed, the lizard turned into a pygmy **dragon**! It was pretty small but it had big teeth. Cordelia was very scared. She turned and started to run, but looked back. The dragon was crying. Cordelia turned to it. When she came near, the dragon backed away. Cordelia came closer and closer.

'My name is Cordelia,' she said. 'What is yours?'

'Al-Al-Al-g-g-gernon,' he stuttered. He was still crying.

'What's wrong?' asked Cordelia.

'I have a thistle in my foot.'

Cordelia looked at his foot. There was a big prickle in it and she pulled it out. When it came out, Algernon fell backwards into a pond that was nearby.

'Help!'

Cordelia ran to pull him out.

The Thistle Queen heard Algernon cry 'Help!' and rushed down, throwing magic thistles at them.

Just in the nick of time, Cordelia grabbed Algernon and flew over the fence, but he slipped and fell to the ground. The Thistle Queen was almost breathing on them. Cordelia flew down to get him but her hands were too slippery to pick him up. She wrapped her tail around him and flew over the wall of invisibility.

'Thanks for saving me,' said Algernon. 'The Thistle Queen wanted me to destroy people but I don't like hurting living things.'

The Thistle Queen couldn't fly, so she stopped chasing them. **'Thieves, trespassers, troublemakers!'** she yelled.

Cordelia was too tired to fly home so they stopped under an apple tree, ate some apples and went to sleep. In the morning they made a plan to trap the evil Queen.

'I know some of the evil Queen's secrets, and one of them is that if you knock down all her thistles, she is powerless. Her magic is gone,' said Algernon.

'The Thistle Queen has a wall of invisibility all around her palace except on top, doesn't she?' said Cordelia. 'OK then, we'll destroy all her thistles and when she comes out she'll have lost all her power. We'll trap her in the corner of her garden and bring her to the Fairy Headquarters and collect our reward.'

* * ✳ * *

Back at the Thistle Queen's palace, Cordelia and Algernon began whacking thistles down with their tails. It really hurt and their tails were full of prickles, but it was worth it because just as they knocked the last thistle down, the evil Queen came out of her palace.

'What are you doing?' she shrieked, but her voice was barely a whisper.

Cordelia and Algernon trapped the Thistle Queen and took her to Fairy Headquarters. Just as they were about to put her into gaol (she was fading away by the second and had got so small that Cordelia could have put her into her pocket), she turned into a single thistle seed and floated away. I guess you're wondering what happened to the evil Queen. Well, that's a secret.

'Thank you for catching the Thistle Queen,' the Chief of Police said. 'We could never have thought of such a clever plan. Here is your reward, a hundred gold pieces and the secret reward is that you get one wish. Seeing as there are two of you, you may have one wish each.'

Cordelia wished that her grandmother would have good health and Algernon whispered his wish to the Chief of Police.

'Your wishes will be granted in the morning, but you must sleep soundly tonight.'

That was no problem, because they were both very tired and would have done that anyway. Cordelia and Algernon said thank you to the Chief of Police and went home to Cordelia's house. In the morning, her grandma's arthritis had completely vanished. Cordelia got out of bed and started looking for Algernon, but he was nowhere to be seen. There was a knock at the door. Cordelia opened it. There was a handsome young fairy man there.

'Who are you?' said Cordelia. She noticed that he had a green scaly tail. 'Algernon, is that you?'

Cordelia and Algernon got married and lived happily ever after because they both had fairy tails. And always remember, this is the only true Fairy **TAIL**.

The End